DEMI'S
DRAGONS
AND
FANTASTIC CREATURES

by Demi

Henry Holt and Company • **New York**

The Creative Dragon

Tap
heavenly powers
and you'll find
this dragon's moving
through your
mind.

The
Water
Dragon

He sleeps
in the sea and
flies to the sky.
His goodness flows
to all
nearby!

The Phoenix

The
phoenix
is the dragon's wife.
She helps him right
the wrongs
of life.

The Unicorn

If you find a unicorn— luck, long life, and joy are born!

The Tortoise

The
tortoise gives
power to the mind.
Enduring and strong,
he's wise and
kind.

Courageous,
fierce, grand, and stern—
if demons come,
he'll make them turn!

The Tiger

The
Fire
Dragon

The Mountain Dragon

Great and graceful, quiet and firm— this dragon's lesson is wise to learn.

Fiery dragon—
blazing bright.
Dancing dragon—
lights the night!

Merry
and playful,
loyal and true,
this little dog brings
riches to you!

The Butterfly Lion Dog

The Lioness

The lioness fights
for wisdom and truth;
she scares away demons
with claw and tooth.

The Elephant

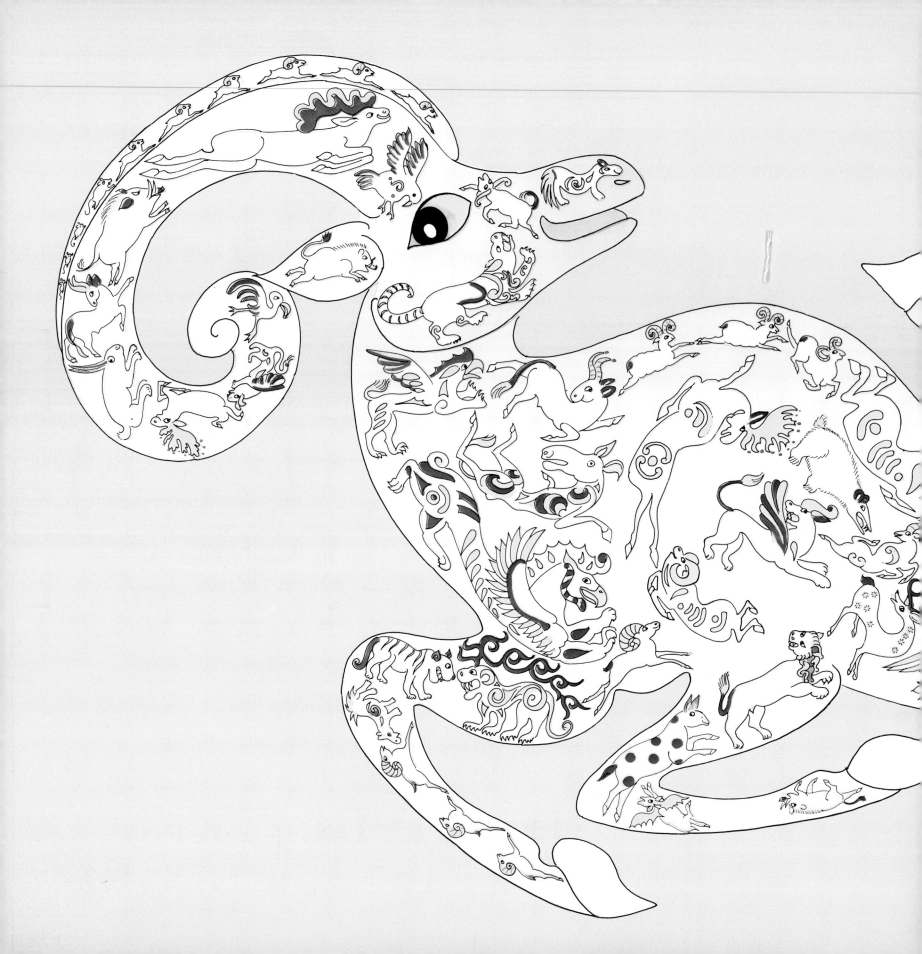

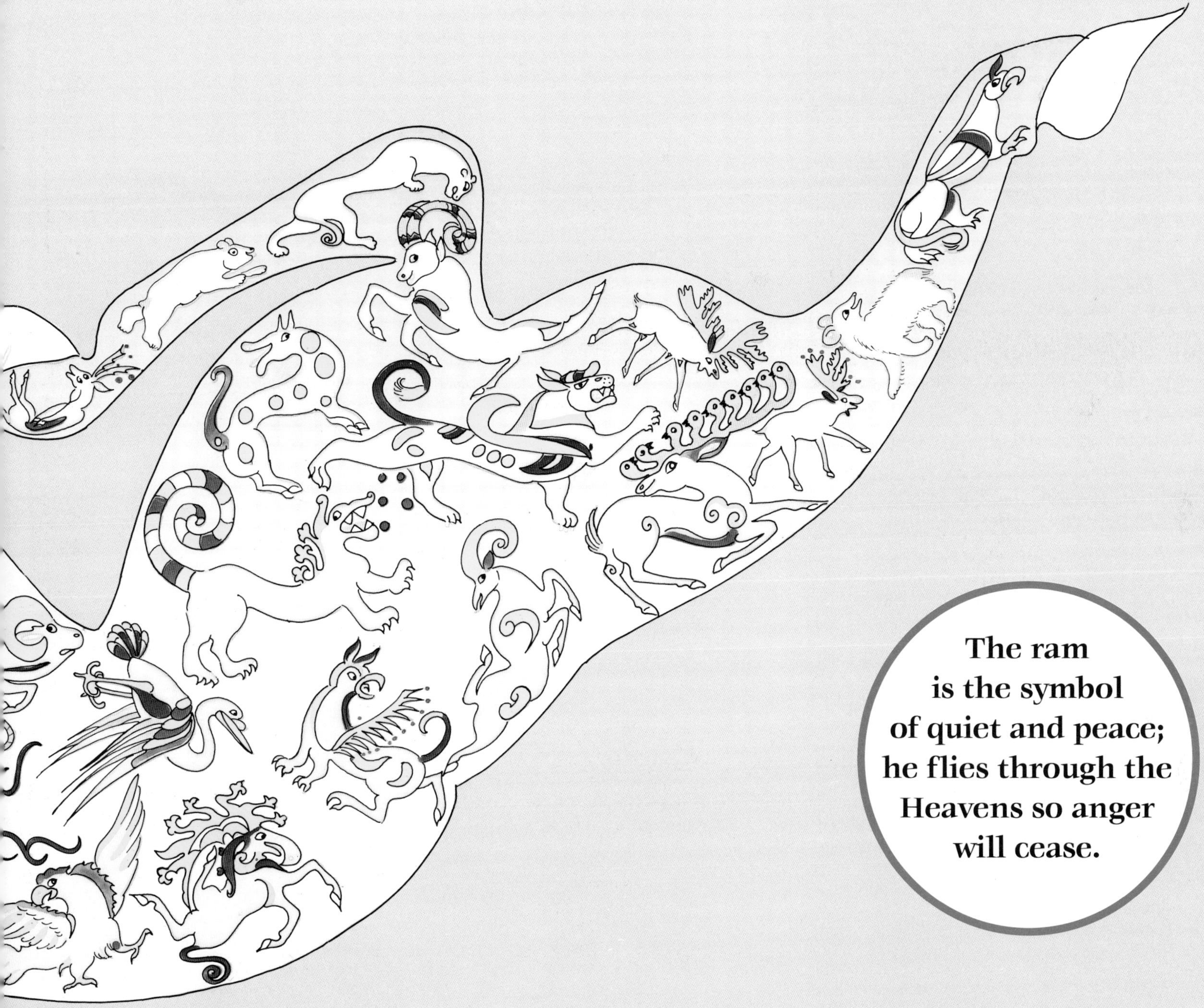

The ram
is the symbol
of quiet and peace;
he flies through the
Heavens so anger
will cease.

The Flying Ram

The
Thunder
Dragon

Sweeping
the mind free
and clean,
sweeping gently,
deeply,
wisdom's seen!

Sleeping soundly his powers concealed, awakened suddenly they're loudly revealed!

The
Wind Dragon

The Guardians

Protecting
the earth from
anger and greed,
these guardians prowl
so all will be
freed.

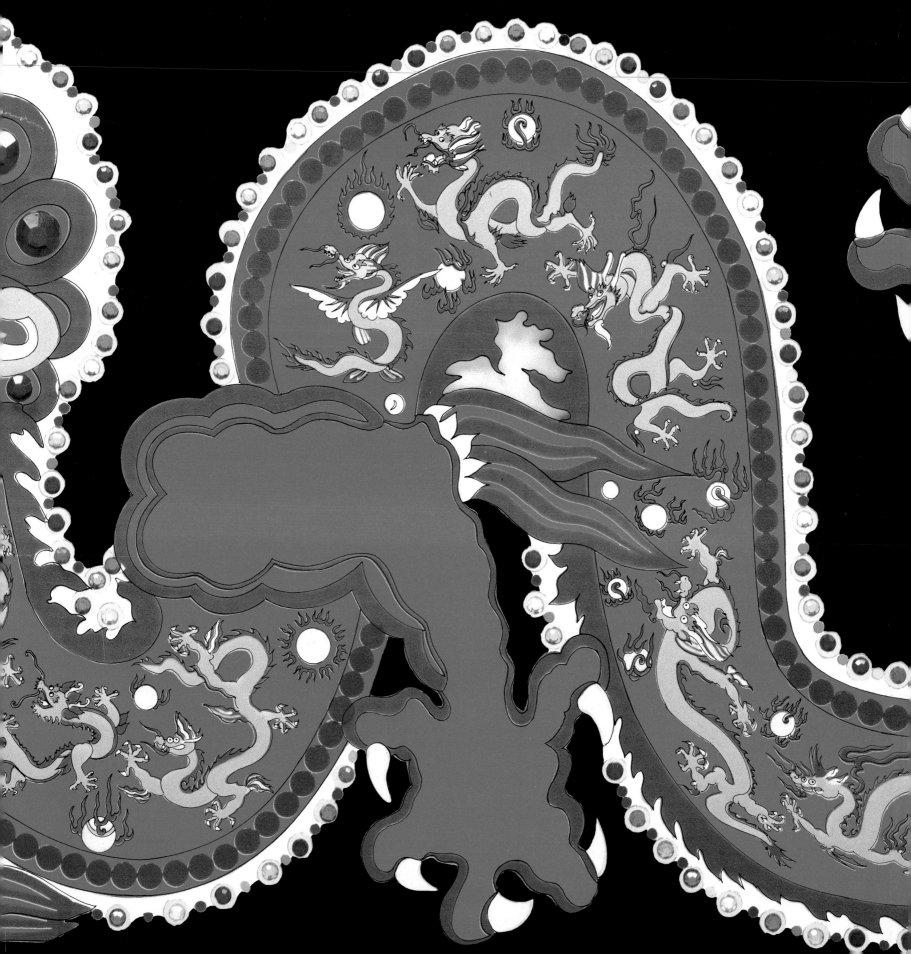

The Heavenly Dragon
flies everywhere—
on the earth—
in our minds—
in our hearts—
in our prayers!

The Earth Dragon

Receptive
and calm,
yielding and blithe,
the Earth Dragon
gives all
beauty and life.

The
Heavenly
Dragon

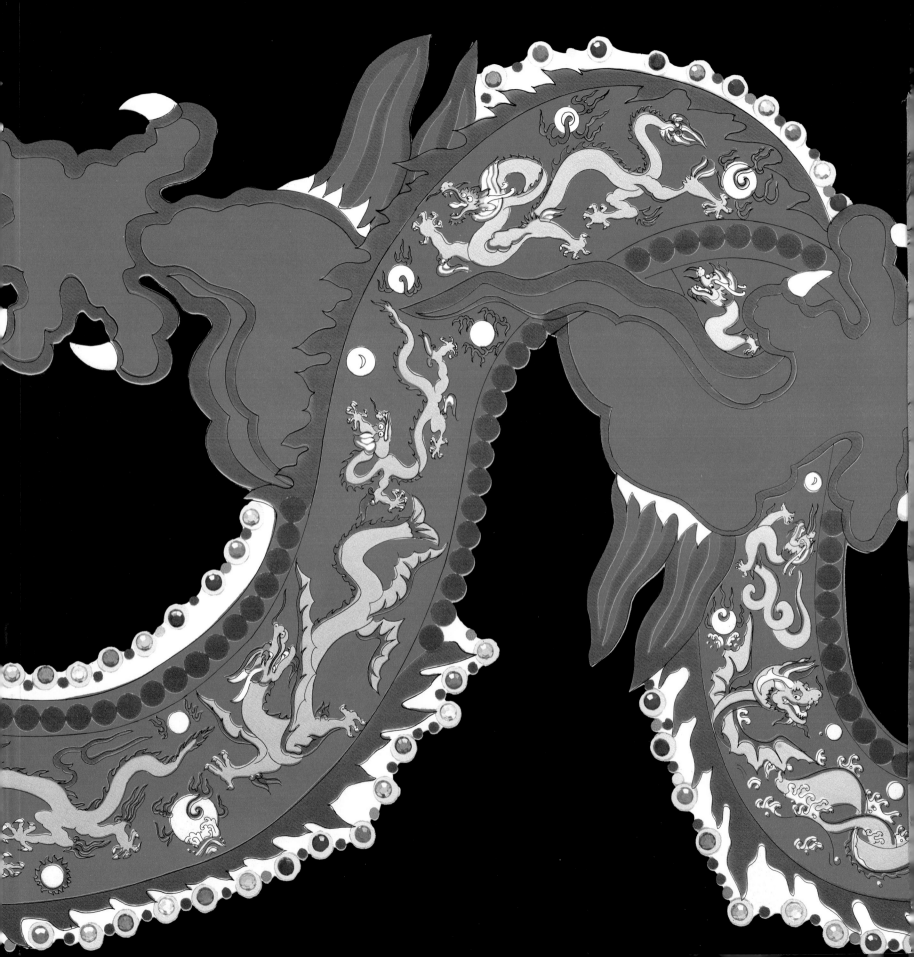

The Lake Dragon

As joyful lakes are fed by brooks, so knowledge feeds our minds by books.

The Chinese dragon is the symbol of all that is good in traditional Chinese culture—peace, courage, wealth, wisdom, and power. In contrast to the Western dragon, which is usually depicted as a horrible, fire-breathing monster, the fantastic Chinese dragons and their related mythological creatures are the embodiment of good spirits.

The magical dragon is able to assume many forms both visible and invisible. He can hide in the caves of inaccessible mountains, or lie coiled in the unfathomed depths of the sea. He unfolds himself in gathering storm clouds and washes his black mane in the darkest of whirlpools. From his claws come jolts of lightning and from his scales, the bark of trees. Chinese dragons are often depicted chasing a sphere that represents the mystical pearl of wisdom.

The dragon is one of the most used motifs in China's rich culture and arts. The dragon was the symbol of the emperor, the Son of Heaven, and appeared on both his richly embroidered robes and in the imperial coat of arms as two dragons protecting the pearl of wisdom. On Chinese New Year and at wedding feasts the dragon dances are celebrated. The Chinese word for dragon (*long*) is often compounded with other words to name towns, rivers, and mountains. (The town of Kowloon—Jiulong in Mandarin—is the "town of the nine dragons.") But whether depicted as architectural detail or embellishment to fine tapestries, or as the dragons of Taoist paintings that give substance to the idea of *ch'i* (energy), the Chinese dragon is always a mighty, mysterious, profound creature.

The Creative Dragon is the symbol of progress. He is multicolored and strong, spirited, persevering, moderate, pure.

The Water Dragon gives rise to all life on earth. But beware! If awakened from sleep, the Water Dragon turns a violent somersault and flies to the sky. His colors are blue and white.

The Phoenix is the dragon's beautiful and virtuous wife. Empress to all the birds, she is attended by a train of small birds at all times. She is considerate of all living things and never pecks insects or tramples on plants. Her favorite color is red for the Vermilion Hills, where she lives waiting for peace to rule the earth.

The Unicorn is the fabulous creature of good omen. He represents longevity, happiness, illustrious offspring, justice and law. He is gaily colored and has a voice like the tinkling of bells. One would be very fortunate to see a Chinese unicorn.

The Tortoise, symbol of winter, lives in the northern quadrant of the heavens. His dome-shaped back represents the vault of the sky; his belly represents the earth that moves upon the waters. His markings correspond to the constellations. His color is green.

Lord of all the animals, the Tiger rules with dignity and courage. His presence means danger as he scares all demons and evil spirits away. His colors, yellow and orange, express his fierce nature.

The Fire Dragon's color is bright, fiery red. He is radiant, serious and composed. But most of all, he is brightest of the bright.

The Mountain Dragon is everything that is tranquil and quiet. Still and graceful, he embodies a great heart with a taming power. The Mountain Dragon's color is purple and blue.

The Butterfly Lion Dog is bright and cheerful. He makes a good friend—affectionate without selfishness, playful without malice, faithful without deceit.

The Lioness, defender of the law, wards off evil spirits. She is a symbol of valor, energy and wisdom, and her color is gold.

The Elephant, a colossal earth-shaking beast, has six tusks. He symbolizes strength, sagacity, and power. His colors are purple and pink.

The Flying Ram represents filial piety, symbolized by the young goat kneeling respectfully when it takes its mother's milk. His colors are white and blue.

The Thunder Dragon is electrically charged with a great arousing, dynamic force. In winter he sleeps in the earth, but in summer he is awake and loudly active in the sky. His color is black.

The Wind Dragon is the complement of the zephyrs in Western literature. He is gentle, innocent, penetrating, and always increasing. His color is silver.

Mighty soldiers of the dragon, the Guardians protect his law. They are on constant guard watching for fires and natural disasters. Their colors are red.

The Earth Dragon's color is green, and, like his color, is mild, devoted, and calm. He is the power of nature that nourishes all living things, giving them beauty and splendor.

The Heavenly Dragon is all power—primal, energetic, and regenerative. Active and strong-spirited, he is the symbol of harmony, peace, security, wealth, and wisdom. He has the power of time, so he is enduring, persevering, and always successful. He is everything, everywhere: simultaneously invisible and visible as all the colors in the rainbow.

The Lake Dragon is personified by his color blue and is joyous, sparkling, and smiling.

The Baby Dragon represents the dragon's eggs, which take one thousand years to hatch. When they do hatch, they are accompanied by rain, lightning, and darkness. His color is sparkling color.

**The little dragon
born this hour
brings
wealth and wisdom
truth and power!**

**For Charlotte
and
Harrison E. Salisbury**

Henry Holt and Company, Inc.
Publishers since 1866
115 West 18th Street
New York, New York 10011

Henry Holt is a registered
trademark of Henry Holt and Company, Inc.

Published in Canada by Fitzhenry & Whiteside Ltd.,
195 Allstate Parkway, Markham, Ontario L3R 4T8.

A CIP catalog record for this book is available.

ISBN 0-8050-2564-2

First Edition—1993

Printed in Hong Kong

1 3 5 7 9 10 8 6 4 2